# Advertisements

Julie Haydon

**Kittens for Sale**

3 females, 2 males
10 weeks old, grey fur,
beautiful and friendly.
$50 each.
ph: 0500 1999.

## Chapter 1

# Kittens for Sale

Leah's cat has had kittens.
Leah cannot keep the kittens,
so she wants to sell them.

Leah's dad helps her to write an ad. The word 'ad' is short for **advertisement**. They put the ad in the newspaper. They have to pay money to do this.

Kittens for Sale

3 females, 2 males
10 weeks old, grey fur,
beautiful and friendly.
$50 each.
ph: 0500 1999.

People who want kittens
read the ad in the newspaper.
They phone Leah's dad and make a time
to come and see the kittens.

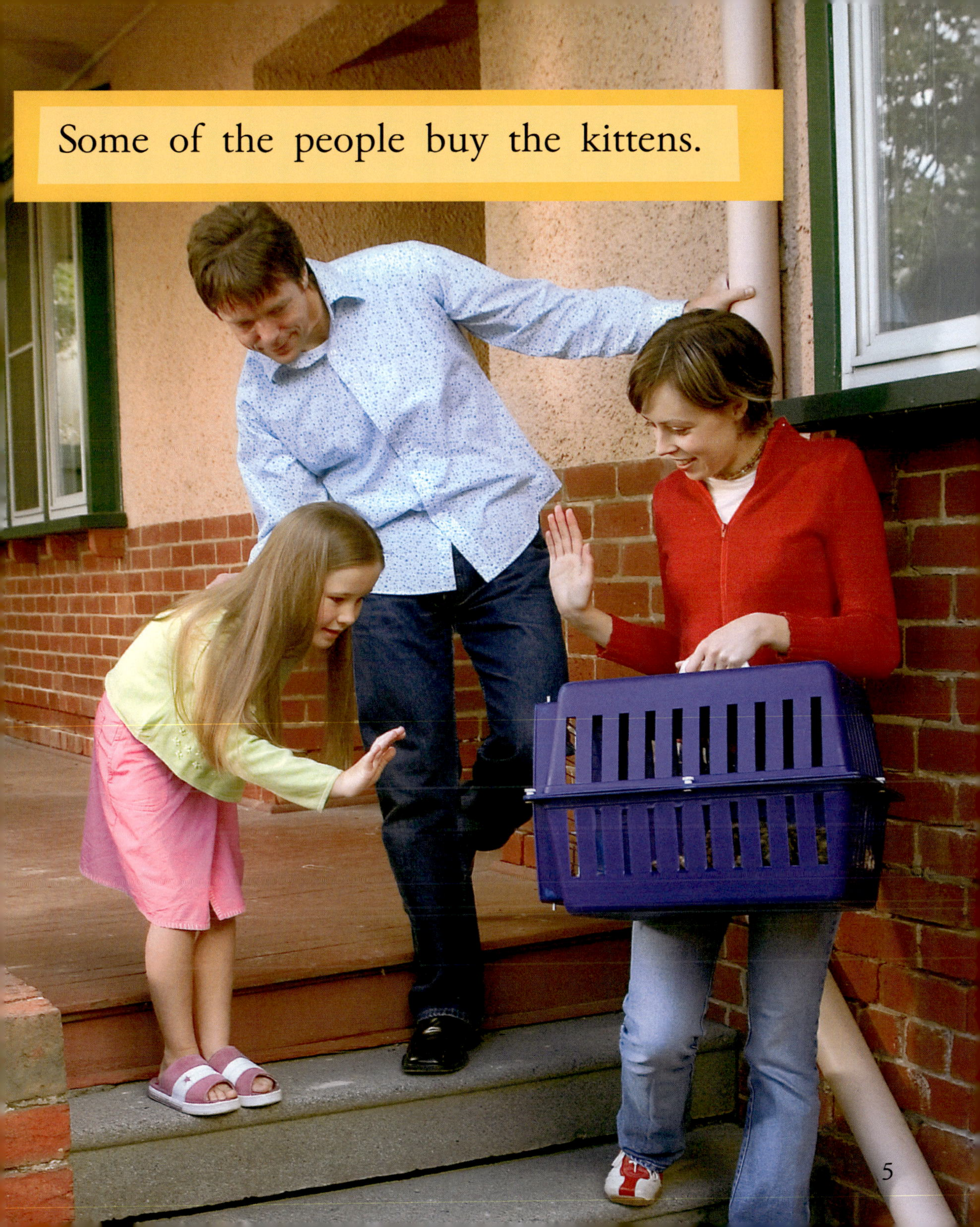

Some of the people buy the kittens.

Chapter 2

# What Is an Ad?

An ad is a **message**.
It lets people know something.

People pay for ads
when they have something to sell.

Chapter 3

# All Around Us

Ads are all around us.

You can hear ads on the radio, and see ads on the television and at the cinema.

an ad on a billboard

You can see ads
on the street,
in shopping malls
and on the **Internet**.

You can see ads in newspapers and magazines.

Some ads are put in your letter box.

Chapter 4

# Making Ads

Some ads are made by people who work at an **advertising agency.**

The people at the advertising agency must:

- think up the ad
- make the ad
- put the ad where people will see or hear it.

making an ad for television

The money for an ad comes from the people who want the ad made.
They are called **advertisers**.
Advertisers pay money
to the advertising agency.

Chapter 5

# Kinds of Ads

There are lots of kinds of ads.

This ad has lots of words in it. The words tell you about the thing, or **product**, that is for sale.

## Her first six months will decide her whole life.

A tiny kitten is a big responsibility, with even bigger rewards. You'll marvel at the speed she develops. If she was a baby she'd be at university by the time she was two-and-a-half. That's why we developed a food specially to provide for all the nutritional needs of a growing kitten.

And now, we've gone even further – we're giving her and you a choice. Three specially prepared new varieties – Rabbit, Chicken and Cod.

All have the necessary proteins and calories she requires in an easily digestible form for a stomach as tiny as the tip of your thumb. And because her bones are growing every day, the new varieties also contain the perfect ratio of phosphorous to calcium to make them strong.

Whiskas® Kitten Food.
Right from the start, Whiskas® cares for her better.

an ad for cat food

This ad has a big photo in it, but only a few words.

Richard Branson
age $3\frac{1}{4}$

an ad for Play-Doh

For years kids have made it with Play-Doh.

Ads on the radio, television and at the cinema have voices and sounds in them.
Some ads have music too.

a television ad with music

Chapter 6

# How Ads Work

Most ads are made
because advertisers want you to buy a product.

Advertisers want you to:

- see or hear their ad
- watch, read or listen to their ad
- like the product in their ad
- buy their product.

Most ads for children's products are full of colour and sounds. The ads make the products look like they would be fun to have.

an ad for breakfast cereal

Do not buy something
just because you like the ad.
Think carefully first.
Ask your mum or dad
if the product is any good.
How much do you want it or need it?

Chapter 7

# Make Your Own Ad

You can make an ad for a new chocolate bar, called *Choccy Bar*.

You will need:

- paper
- coloured pens.

1. Plan the words or pictures for your ad.
2. Write and draw the words or pictures.
3. Put the ads up around the classroom!

# Glossary

| | |
|---|---|
| **advertisement** | a message that people pay for, so that other people will see or hear it |
| **advertisers** | people who pay for ads |
| **advertising agency** | a business that makes ads for advertisers |
| **Internet** | lots of computers that are linked together and share information |
| **message** | information that is sent or shown to people |
| **product** | a thing that is made. Most products are sold to people. |

# Index